Doctor Hurtz

On one side of the world, which was called The Old World, under a big tree, there was a clinic for animals. The doctor there was Doctor Hurtz. Doctor Hurtz was a very kind person, who would treat every sick animal, no matter how big or how small. A cow would come to him for help, and a she-wolf, and a bug, and even a worm, and also a bear! Whoever called for his help, saying: "Doctor! Hurts!", the kind Doctor Hurtz would immediately check what the hurt was, prescribe the best treatment, and cure them all.

Animal Clinic of Dr. Hurtz

The clinic of Doctor Hurtz was very busy. He had many-many patients. One day, for example, a fox came to see the doctor in the morning, crying. "Doctor, hurts!" she said, "I was stung by a wasp." The doctor examined the hurt and applied to it a very cool compress. The fox barely left and already another patient was coming: a dog. The dog tried to be friendly to little chicks, but their mother, the hen, did not want her children to talk to strangers and pecked the dog very painfully on the nose. Doctor Hurtz bandaged the nose and it did not hurt anymore.

The dog wagged his tail to show the doctor how grateful he was, but was interrupted by the Mother Rabbit, who ran into the clinic in tears, sobbing piteously: "Oh, woe is me! My little bunny-boy was in an accident. He played on the road – ah, ah! – and did not notice the approaching car! And now his legs are so hurt, and he is lame and in pain! My darling little Bunny – he will never run again."

The doctor comforted the poor mother, saying to her: "Don't worry, Mother Rabbit, just bring little Bunny here, and I shall make his legs as good as new. He won't even remember that he had an accident." And the lame little

bunny-boy was brought to the clinic. He was so sick that other animals wept, looking at him. But Doctor Hurtz carefully and quickly sewed his legs back in place, giving him sweet medicine to make him stronger, and by the end of the day Bunny was hopping and dancing again.

Animal Clinic of Dr. Hurtz

Chocolate

3

One day animals noticed the mail-jackal, riding his postal mare at full gallop. In his paw was something that looked like a very urgent message. Arriving at the clinic the jackal said: "A very urgent message to Doctor Hurtz from Hyppopotamus."

The text of the message was: "Doctor Hurtz, come as soon as you can to New Zooland on the other side of the world to save our children."

Without waiting a moment, Doctor Hurtz texted back: "What is the problem? Could it be that your children are ill?"

"Yes. Yes. And Yes," was the response. "They caught all the children's diseases. Everything hurts. So, please, kind Doctor Hurtz, come as soon as possible."

"Of course, of course," texted the doctor, "I am coming. But what is your address in New Zooland? Do you live on a mountain or in a swamp?" "We live on the desert shores of the Big Ocean, in Hippo-poppo-country. Remember, you must come running."

4

So Doctor Hurtz got up, quickly packed his medical bag, and ran out of the clinic on his side of the world. All the while he was repeating, so as not to forget the address of the sick animals in New Zooland: "Hippo-poppo, Hippo-poppo, Hippo-poppo."

In the meantime, winter came to the Old World, where Dr. Hurtz lived. As the kind doctor ran, wind, snow, and hail blew into his face and advised him: "Hey, Hurtz, you better turn back, this is not a good time to travel." Indeed, Doctor Hurtz fell and thought to himself, as he lay in the snow: "No, I cannot run any further."

But a bunny, who was running alongside Doctor Hurtz, to report to other animals on the progress of his journey, texted about what happened and birds retweeted the news of the fall all over the forest. As a result, the moment the doctor thought so, two wolves rushed to him from behind a fir-tree and said in rough voices, but with the best intentions: "Come on, Hurtz, sit astride, and we'll quickly deliver you to the end of this side of the world." Doctor Hurtz climbed on the back of one wolf, while the other offered to carry his heavy medical bag, and they were on their way.

All the while, so as not to forget, Doctor Hurtz was repeating to himself:

"Hippo-poppo, Hippo-poppo, Hippo-poppo."

Soon the wolves, who can run very fast, reached the shores of the Big Ocean which separates one side of the world from the other. The Big Ocean was stormy. Large waves threatened to swallow Doctor Hurtz with his medical bag, and knapsack, and umbrella. "What will happen," thought the doctor, "with the sick wild animals in New Zooland, if I go to the bottom and drown?"

In answer to his thoughts, a whale rose from the depths of the Big Ocean (for he was following the news and was well aware of the arrival of Doctor Hurtz on the shore) and said: "Please, dear Doctor, consider my wide back your special ship, and I'll carry you across to the other side of the world."

And Doctor Hurtz settled comfortably on the back of the whale with all his baggage, all the while repeating to himself "Hippo-poppo," so as not to forget the address of his patients.

When the whale reached the shores of New Zooland, however, great mountains stood on the way of Doctor Hurtz. He started climbing them, which, with his bag and umbrella, was not easy, and again worried: "If I fall from these mountains or get lost, what will happen with the poor sick animals who are waiting for me?" He never thought about himself, only about the animals who needed his help!

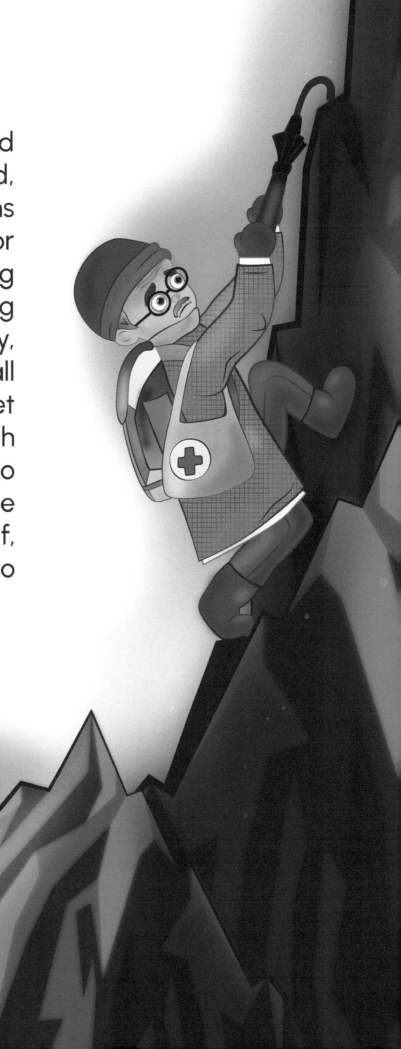

Doctor Hurtz hardly had the time, however, to think that worried thought, when a whole fleet of eagles came down from the highest rock and also offered to him their backs: "Sit astride, Hurtz," they said, "we'll carry you over the mountains."

Still constantly repeating to himself "Hippo-poppo, Hippo-poppo," Doctor Hurtz climbed on the back of an eagle and they took off.

At that time in New Zooland in Hippo-poppo-country a very sad hippopotamus was sitting and crying bitterly. He was sitting under a palm tree and without rest looking and looking at the Big Ocean from the shore to see if Doctor Hurtz was finally arriving. Elephants and rhinos prowled hither and thither, angrily mumbling: "Hurtz! Hurtz! Where is this vaunted Doctor Hurtz, who they say helps every animal that hurts? Why doesn't he come to help children of New Zooland"?

On the shore of the Big Ocean lay several little hippopotami, holding on to their tummies: these little hippopotami had a terrible tummy ache. Not far from them a group of ostrich chicks squealed like little piglets: they were delirious and forgot proper Ostrich language. No wonder! They had all children's diseases at once, and in addition suffered from a terrible headache and sore throat. "Hurts, hurts!" they raved, "Why isn't Doctor Hurtz coming? Hurts, hurts!"

A Great White shark was lying nearby with eyes full of tears. Her little baby sharks were suffering from toothache for a full twelve days. Their moans broke her mother's heart and drove her up the rocks.

Even a little grasshopper – barely a toddler – was ill: he had a dislocated shoulder. He could neither hop nor skip and piteously cried: "Oh, where is the kind doctor? Why is he not coming? Hurts, hurts…"

Suddenly, a very large bird was perceived in the sky. It was coming closer and closer to the shores of Hippo-poppo. Astride the bird sat a man with an umbrella, in whom everyone immediately recognized Doctor Hurtz. He was waving his hat and loudly shouting: "Long live New Zooland!"

All the children on the shore and their parents were jubilant: "He came! He came!" they shouted, "Hooray, hooray!"

The eagle landed and Doctor Hurtz ran to the little hippopotami, touched their tummies, and, understanding what was wrong with them, put all of them in bed and administered to each little hippopotamus a chocolate. This was the special medicine Doctor Hurtz used for tummy aches. After that he measured their temperatures. "I am so glad," he thought, "that I brought so many thermometers in my bag: every sick animal likes the cool touch of a thermometer once in a while."

Finished with hippopotami, Doctor Hurtz ran to other animals. and, since he very soon ran out of chocolate, he administered to them other sweet medicines. In the end all the medicines the kind doctor brought in his bag were gone. Fortunately, there were plenty of thermometers.

For ten whole days and ten whole nights, during which Doctor Hurtz did not sleep, he tended to the sick animal children, constantly, tirelessly measuring their temperature.

And what do you think? After ten days and ten nights all the sick animal children were cured! They were healthy and happy again, and they laughed and danced and played. Especially happy were the little hippopotami. They slapped their healthy tummies and veritably roared with laughter.

And their father Hippopotamus, who sent the message to Doctor Hurtz, asking him to come from the Old World to New Zooland, now sent messages all over the world, telling everyone how Doctor Hurtz saved the children of Hippo-poppo-country. And the birds tweeted and re-tweeted. "Glory to kind animal doctors!!! Glory to the ve-te-ri-narians!!!"

Letter to Parents and Teachers of Little Kids

It is difficult to find books that can help little children to choose what they want to be when they grow up. With so many grownups around them struggling with their identities, with so many choices, and so little knowledge, preschoolers today need such help. To develop their selves and decide who they are, they need simple, non-confrontational ideals. That's why, after decades of study and writing about our complex society, which makes identity-formation so problematic, I decided to create a series of books for very young children.

"Miss Buzzz, the Fly" and the four stories following it: "Doctor Hurtz," "The Giant Cockroach," "Topsy-Turvy," and "The Stolen Sun" are prose stories adapted from the rhymed tales in Russian by Korney Chukovsky, a great children's literature writer and student of child psychology, written about a hundred years ago.

For generations these stories provided a moral compass to little Russians, Ukrainians, Georgians, Kazakh, and others, often forced to grow up in confusing and scary times. Now, as we, too, are caught up in confusing and scary times, they may be particularly helpful for little Americans and other English-speakers. Chukovsky's goal in writing was to teach a child how to be **a good person, above all else,** to cultivate in the child kindness (humane disposition) and empathy, "this marvelous ability to worry about other people's misfortunes, to rejoice at other people's joys, and to experience another person's destiny as one's own." A good person would focus on others, not on oneself, and have courage to help the helpless and defend the defenseless whenever such help and defense could be needed. A truly bad person, in distinction, would be someone who intentionally hurt someone else. There are wonderful role models for children in Chukovsky's stories: from a dashing brave mosquito, who saves a hapless fly from the clutches of a cruel spider to a selfless veterinarian Dr. Hurtz, who crosses the world to cure little animals in a far-off corner from numerous childhood diseases.

The child learns that anyone can be a good person, no matter whether one has six legs, four legs, two legs, or no legs at all. And there are also models of what one should not be: cowardly animals, believing rumors about and hiding from a giant cockroach, who turns on inspection to be a regular insect on skinny legs and, as such, eaten by a sparrow; insects, thinking only about their own safety and abandoning Miss Buzzz, whose friends they pretended to be in good times, in her hour of need; silly kittens who decide on a whim to oink like piglets and set the blue sea on fire, or selfish folk, who would not move a claw or a hoof to save the sun from the Crocodile who stole it, but expect the old grandfather Bear to do this for them.

All the stories have a happy ending, because good persons always win and are celebrated by the multitude.

Printed in the USA
CPSIA information can be obtained
at www.ICGtesting.com
LVHW061808020124
767889LV00017B/252